Mrs. Rosey-Posey

and the Chocolate Cherry Treat

Robin Jones Gunn
Illustrated by Bill Duca

"If you stay away from sin you will
be like one of these dishes made of
purest gold–the very best in the
house–so that Christ himself can
use you for his highest purposes."
II Timothy 2:21 (TLB)

Chariot Books™
David C. Cook Publishing Co

Especially for Natalie Olivia Hendrix, the "fine china plate"
who inspired this story
R.J.G.

To my parents, Allan and Patricia Duca
B.D.

Chariot Books™ is an imprint of David C. Cook Publishing Co.
David C. Cook Publishing Co., Elgin, Illinois 60120
David C. Cook Publishing Co., Weston, Ontario
MRS. ROSEY-POSEY AND THE CHOCOLATE CHERRY TREAT
©1991 by Robin Jones Gunn for text and Bill Duca for illustrations

Designed by Donna Kae Nelson
First Printing, 1991
Printed in Singapore
95 94 93   5 4 3

Library of Congress Cataloging-in-Publication Data
Gunn, Robin Jones,
      Mrs. Rosey-Posey and the chocolate cherry treat/ Robin Jones Gunn;
[illustrated by Bill Duca].
             p.   cm. — (On my own books)
      Summary: Natalie learns a lesson about making choices from Mrs. Rosey-
Posey who also introduces a Bible verse from the second book of Timothy.
      ISBN 1-55513-370-3
      [1. Choice--Fiction. 2. Conduct of life--Fiction. 3. Christian Life--
Fiction.]   I. Duca, Bill, ill. II Title.
PZ7.G972Mq 1990
E--dc20   89-25417
                                                          CIP

Verses marked (TLB) are taken from The Living Bible ©1971, owned
by assignment by Illinois Regional Bank N.A. (as trustee). Used by
permission of Tyndale House Publishers Inc., Wheaton, IL 60189.
All rights reserved.

Poppyville

Right in the middle of Poppyville, at the end of Marigold Lane, stands a big, yellow house.

All the children in Poppyville love this house.

They love to play in the attic. They love to roller-skate on the porch. And they love to feed the ducks in the pond.

But what the children love most about
this house is Mrs. Rosey-Posey. She has a
thousand secrets. When she gets a
twinkle-sparkle-zing look in her eyes, she
is about to give away one of those secrets.

One sunny Saturday, Mrs. Rosey-Posey
saw Natalie sitting on her porch swing.

"Mercy me!" cried Mrs. Rosey-Posey.
"Such a frown! Whatever is the matter,
Natalie Olivia?"

Mrs. Rosey-Posey always calls the children by their first two names. Not the way your mother does when she's upset with you. But it's like she's calling you "Prince" or "Princess."

"It's not fair!" Natalie told Mrs. Rosey-Posey. "All my friends went to the movies without me."

"Why?" asked Mrs. Rosey-Posey.

"My mom and dad said I could not go. They said it was not the kind of movie I should see."

"And your friends went anyway?" Mrs. Rosey-Posey asked.

"Yes," said Natalie. "My parents were the only parents who said no."

"Mercy me!" said Mrs. Rosey-Posey, shaking her head. "You are right. That is not fair to your friends at all!"

"What?" Natalie cried. "What do you mean it is not fair to my friends? I think it is not fair to me!"

Natalie looked at Mrs. Rosey-Posey. She had that twinkle-sparkle-zing look in her eyes.

"Natalie Olivia," she said. "Did you know that you have been set apart? Your parents are helping you make the right choice."

"Set apart?" Natalie said. "What does that mean?"

"Come with me," said Mrs. Rosey-Posey. She took Natalie by the hand.

"Natalie Olivia," she said. "You are about to learn the secret of the fine china plate."

And off they marched to the kitchen.

"This morning I picked cherries," said Mrs. Rosey-Posey. "Then I dipped them in chocolate. Would you like some?"

"Oh, yes!" said Natalie.

Mrs. Rosey-Posey pulled a dirty paper plate out of the trash. "Would you like me to put your cherries on this plate?" Mrs. Rosey-Posey asked with a smile.

"Well," said Natalie, "if that is all you have. . . . "

"Goodness, no!" said Mrs. Rosey-
Posey. "I have other plates. Clean plates.
Special plates. Plates which I have kept set
apart."

They went into the dining room.
Natalie sat down. Mrs. Rosey-Posey put
three plates in front of her.

First, the dirty paper plate.

Then a plain, brown dinner plate.

Then a beautiful, fine china plate with gold trim.

"Which plate would you like to use for your cherries?" Mrs. Rosey-Posey asked.

"This one," Natalie said. She pointed to the fine china plate.

Mrs. Rosey-Posey scooped the cherries on to it. "Why did you pick this one?" she asked.

"Well, the paper plate was dirty,"
Natalie explained. "The dinner plate was
boring. But this one is beautiful."

"Indeed!" said Mrs. Rosey-Posey. She sat down next to Natalie. "Now I shall tell you the story of the fine china plate."

Natalie popped a cherry in her mouth. She nodded and listened with her heart.

"Once there was a dinner plate. She was young and free. With all her heart she wanted to be special. She wanted to serve the King.

"Her friends called to her one day, 'Come with us! We're going to get smeared with beans and hot dogs!'

"The dinner plate wanted to go. But she thought, *If I were a fine china plate, I would never get smeared with beans and hot dogs.*

" 'I cannot go,' she told her friends. 'I want to keep clean. The King might want to use me someday.'

"Her friends laughed. 'Little Miss Set-Apart thinks she is too good for us.' And they went on without her.

"The dinner plate felt sad. Being set apart is sometimes very lonely.

"Then one day, the King came! He was looking for a clean plate that He could use.

"All the plates lined up.

" 'Pick me! Pick me!' they cried.

"The dinner plate looked at her friends. They were no longer dinner plates! They had turned into paper plates! Dark bean stains covered their sagging edges.

"Suddenly the King reached for the lonely dinner plate. He smiled. 'I am glad you waited for me,' he said. 'I am glad you stayed clean. You made the right choice. I will now turn you into a fine china plate and use you to serve others.' "

Mrs. Rosey-Posey leaned forward. "Do you know what all the paper plates said?"

"No, what?" Natalie asked.

"They shouted, 'It's not fair! Pick us! Turn us into china plates, too!' "

Natalie laughed. "They had a choice. They did not have to get covered with beans and hot dogs. They could have said 'no.' The dinner plate did."

"Mercy me!" said Mrs. Rosey-Posey. "Perhaps they needed someone to help them make the right choice."

"You mean the way my parents helped me today? They wanted me to stay clean. So they said 'no' to the movie."

"Indeed!" said Mrs. Rosey-Posey.

It was quiet for a moment. Then Mrs. Rosey-Posey whispered, "Natalie Olivia, what kind of plate would you like to be?"

Natalie looked into Mrs. Rosey-Posey's dancing eyes. She saw a silver tear.

Natalie sat up. She spoke in a clear voice. "I would like to be a fine china plate. The kind of plate the King can use."

Then Mrs. Rosey-Posey did something
strange. She sang to Natalie. Her voice
was thick and sweet, like a caramel apple.
This is what she sang:

Set apart, just like a fine china plate
Clean and ready to serve the King
Purest gold, with a heart that's true to
   Him
Set apart, the choice is up to you.

Then Mrs. Rosey-Posey took a pen out of her pocket. She picked up Natalie's plate and wrote on the back of it.

"This is for you," Mrs. Rosey-Posey said. "Treasure it always." She handed the china plate to Natalie.

Natalie looked on the back of the plate. It said,

For
Natalie Olivia

Love Always,
Mrs. Rosey-Posey

II Timothy
2:21

"What does II Timothy 2:21 say?" Natalie asked.

"It says, 'If you stay away from sin you will be like one of these dishes made of purest gold—the very best in the house—so that Christ himself can use you for his highest purposes.' "

"Wow!" Natalie said. "You mean the secret of the fine china plate is found in the Bible?"

"Of course!" Mrs. Rosey-Posey said. "That is where all my secrets come from."

Natalie hugged Mrs. Rosey-Posey. "You make me feel so special. How can I ever thank you?"

"Natalie Olivia," said Mrs. Rosey-Posey. "You are special. You are set apart, just like a fine china plate. Stay clean, my dear one. And I promise you, one day the King will use you."

Recipe for Mrs. Rosey-Posey's Chocolate-Covered Cherry Treat

Microwave directions:

1 cup chocolate chips
2 tablespoons vegetable shortening (not butter)

2 cups washed cherries with stems still attached

Ask a grown-up to help you. Place chips and shortening in a microwave-safe bowl. Microwave at 50% power (medium) for 2 minutes. Stir. Then microwave for 1 to 2 minutes more, until chips are shiny and soft. Stir well. Be careful. The chocolate will be hot.

Hold cherries by the stem and dip them into the chocolate, one at a time. Place chocolate-covered cherries on wax paper and let them cool. Then serve them to someone special.